Dear Abigail,

Happy Christmas

Love

Aunty Helen

—x—

To Harriet, Duncan,
and all little explorers C.M.

For Anne, the loveliest,
the scrummiest, the best C.S.

Text copyright © 2000 Catherine Maccabe
Illustrations copyright © 2000 Clive Scruton
This edition copyright © 2000 Lion Publishing

The moral rights of the author and illustrator
have been asserted

Published by
Lion Publishing plc
Sandy Lane West, Oxford, England
www.lion-publishing.co.uk
ISBN 0 7459 4159 1 (hardback)
ISBN 0 7459 4460 4 (paperback)

First hardback edition 2000
10 9 8 7 6 5 4 3 2 1 0
First paperback edition 2000
10 9 8 7 6 5 4 3 2 1 0

A catalogue record for this book is available
from the British Library

Typeset in 23/32 Garamond ITC
Printed and bound in Singapore

Wednesday 23rd December 2015

Teddy Bear, Piglet, Kitten & Me

Words by Catherine Maccabe * Pictures by Clive Scruton

LION
Children's Books

We went to the beach,
where the waves were so wild,

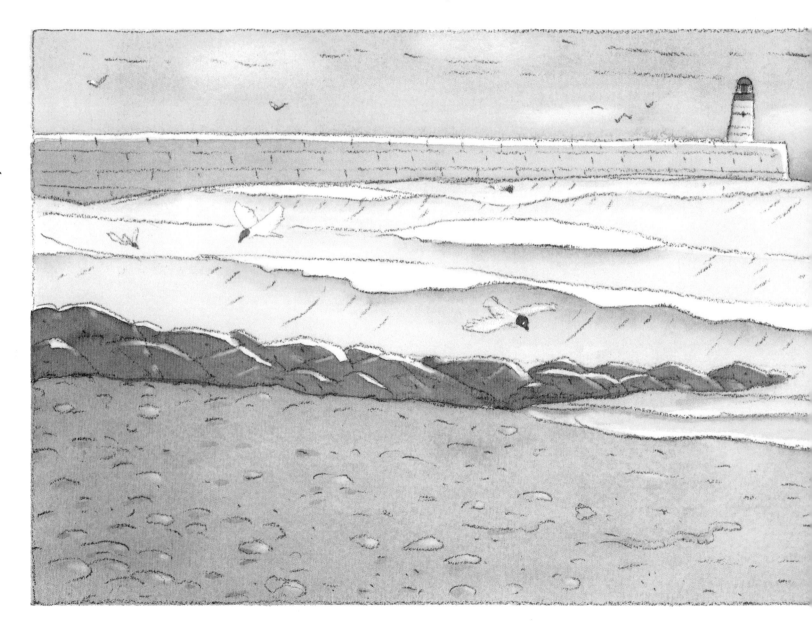

Much larger, dear God,
than one little child:

I know we are small,
but please, can you see,
Teddy bear, piglet,
kitten and me?

We went to the woods,
where the trees grow so high,

I can tell, if I look,
that they reach to the sky:

I know we are small,
but please, can you see,
Teddy bear, piglet,
kitten and me?

We went to the park,
where it started to rain,

There was thunder and lightning
and thunder again:

I know we are small,
but please, can you see,
Teddy bear, piglet,
kitten and me?

We went to the zoo,
where the elephants stay,

They're bigger than houses,
and too big to play:

I know we are small,
but please, can you see,
Teddy bear, piglet,
kitten and me?

We went to the town,
full of bustle and noise,

I nearly got lost
in the shop that sells toys:

I know we are small,
but please, can you see,

Teddy bear, piglet,
kitten and me?

We went to the church,
we walked through the snow,
Inside it was warm
in the candlelit glow:

I know we are small,
but I think you can see,
Teddy bear, piglet,
kitten and me?

We've come to the stable,
we followed the star,
Baby Jesus lies smiling,
we know who you are –

God's son, oh, so small,
so of course you can see,
Teddy bear, piglet,
kitten and me.